Diary of an Evil Queen

A Guide to Living Evilly Ever After

THIS BOOK
BELONGS TO:

Ever After High™

Diary of an

Evil Queen

A Guide to Living
Evilly Ever After

By Stacia Deutsch

LITTLE, BROWN AND COMPANY
New York Boston

Copyright © 2016 Mattel, Inc.

Little, Brown and Company

Hachette Book Group
1290 Avenue of the Americas, New York, NY 10104
Visit us at lb-kids.com

Little, Brown and Company is a division of Hachette Book Group, Inc.
The Little, Brown name and logo are trademarks of
Hachette Book Group, Inc.

The publisher is not responsible for websites (or their content)
that are not owned by the publisher.

First Edition: February 2016

Library of Congress Control Number: 2015951636

ISBN 978-0-316-38995-2

10 9 8 7 6 5 4 3 2 1

RRD-C

Printed in the United States of America

To the Dark Wizard, Jim, and his

Evil Apprentice, Jack. The Evil Queen

would be so proud of you both.

If found, please return this book to the Evil Queen, located in mirror prison, top of tower, Ever After High. Just tap on the glass, and I will gladly appear and reward you handsomely for your efforts.

Dear Raven,

This book is my gift to you. It is my lasting legacy, written from behind the shimmering glass of my mirror prison. From this day forward, I am going to use my time to explain to you how to be an Evil Queen in the hopes that you will someday embrace your destiny and follow in my footsteps.

I don't understand what has gone wrong. From when you were a babe, I taught you everything I know about evil. I was the best mother an up-and-coming Evil Queen could want, and yet, here we are: You have rejected your destiny and, by extension, me. Yes, in your decision to be good, you have turned your back on your mother, the one who raised you, nurtured you, and wiped your cruel little chin.

(Of course, there were nannies who handled most things, but I was there, down in the castle dungeons, hard at work plotting my next evil plan, wondering if your nappies were clean and your chin wiped. And let me assure you, if they weren't—heads would have rolled!)

Now, now, there's no use weeping over the past or what could have been.

This book gives us both a chance to start over. I'll gladly impart all that knowledge to you again because I am your mother and you are my one and only child. Here we go, Raven. We are going to take a fresh stab at Evil 101.

If I hadn't overstepped the boundaries of my own story, invaded Wonderland, and poisoned Sleeping Beauty—even though that was a stroke of evil genius on my part—we'd be sitting side by side on matching thrones, ruling <u>all</u> of Ever After together. I'm not saying what I did wasn't worth it, because it was . . . but the first rule of evil is not to get caught.

Say it with me, Raven: Never get caught.

You must subtly let everyone know that you are behind the act, of course, to build your fame and reputation, but do not let yourself get taken into custody and sent away to prison. Compared to palace living, this place I'm in is an insult.

Harness your evil, Raven, before it's too late. No one ever took over the world by being nice. It's better to be feared than forgotten. I am the ultimate example. How long have I been stuck in this mirror, and yet, I'm still witch and famous! Don't you want to be just like me? Well, the me who isn't wrongly imprisoned, that is.

Here's the worst part of my incarceration: All I need is someone, anyone, to break the mirror, and then I'll be free. Just a light tap on the glass, and I'd be out there, instead of in here. I'd be sweeping through Ever After, hatching evil plots to conquer kingdoms, creating chaos, and working relentlessly to convince you to stand proudly by my side.

Since I cannot be there in person, this book will teach you the rules of evil. You must understand that evil is not something you toss away like fresh flowers. It's not a ridiculous gift like a puppy that you would never, ever want unless you are a simpering fool. (Remember when your father gave you a puppy for your birthday? I don't know what that man was thinking when he did that!) Evil is precious, and it must be honored. Evil must be planted like a seed in the darkest part of your heart and allowed to grow. It must be nurtured until it rots.

Evil is a science. It's a way of life that includes how to dress, what to eat, how to cast dark spells. There is the evil training of dragons and rulers. Evil isn't just one thing. It's everything!

No matter what you may believe, Raven, you and I are not so different. Evil courses through your blood as it does mine. Look in the mirror, and you'll see how similar we are. Take a close look. Closer even. Maybe press your nose against the glass. Yes. Lean right into it. One little step forward, and I will show you how similar we are in person!

Ah well, a mother can dream.

And who knows, maybe one day soon I'll find a way to set myself free.

In the meantime, my precious Raven, if you insist on going off book . . . then this book will come to you.

The Importance
of Evil

Imagine a world without evil. You wake
up in the morning and hear the birds
chirping with their annoying little tweets.
You push aside the headache from that
wretched sound and proceed to the shower,
where hot water is plentiful. When you
emerge, your towel is waiting, warm,
soft, and fuzzy.

Your favorite clothes are laid out, clean, sparkly, and freshly pressed. They fit just right. Your hair falls exactly the way you like it, without weird curls or floppy bangs.

Down in the kitchen, breakfast consists of your favorite foods. You eat fluffy eggs and toast without crusts and delicate doughnuts and crispy bacon and wash it all down with not-too-hot chocolate.

I know this is difficult, but stay with me.

Your day ends with another "perfect" meal, and as you warm your toes by the fire before bed, you think . . .

THIS IS THE WORST DAY EVER!!!!

It's horrible.

Awful.

And you dread doing it all over again the next day. You know you will because all your days are just like this.

How do you wake up from this nightmare?!

Dearest Raven, know this: Without evil, nothing interesting will ever happen. Ever After would be a kingdom of boring princesses and dull princes humming with the birds and smiling their way through bland days of sunshine and rainbows. No evil means no villains. No villains means no heroes. No heroes means no adventures. No more princesses in tall towers, no princes lost in the woods, no daring rescues from giants, and no missions to steal precious jewels from the dragon's lair.

Ever After High would no longer offer classes on potions or beast training, and Mr. Badwolf would be out of a job. Your friends would spend their days learning math, science, and literature! Can you imagine a bleaker future? Math! There's no math in evil... unless of course, you are calculating the diameter of a fire pit and whether that fire would engulf the whole town. Okay, I guess there is <u>some</u> math in evil.

Raven, you must recognize the kind of world you are heading toward.

Think about it.

Do you really want Mr. Badwolf to get FIRED because there's nothing for him to teach? He'll never find another job, and that would be all your fault. For someone who wants so badly to do good, do you really want to be responsible for the poor man wandering through the woods searching for a basket of treats and a soft bed?

Without the sleeping curse, there'd be no Sleeping Beauty.

If not for the poison apple, Snow White would still be living with those dwarves, singing and dancing in their cramped hut.

Hansel and Gretel would have all sorts of poor health issues because the Candy Witch would have just let them devour her entire house. All that sugar is terrible for the teeth! Ah, and then the Candy Witch would be wandering in search of a new home, just like Mr. Badwolf.

And that's just the beginning....

You'd sit down to read a fairytale book and nothing hexciting would happen. Good things would happen to good people, who would all get what they wanted in the end. What hexcitement is there in that?

Honestly, happy dwarves and cheerful flittering bluebirds are only interesting for maybe ten pages. After that, you'd be begging someone to throw a poisoned apple into the story. Begging, I tell you!

Darling Raven, in your quest for goodness, you are missing the point of being evil.

Evil is GOOD for everyone.

Evil brings happiness. More happiness for some, obviously, but still happiness for all! Evil is the key to a Happily Ever After.

There is badness in the world, dear daughter, but is that the fault of evil? Absolutely not. Evil doesn't hurt people. People hurt people.

Think about it: Evil is a big part of that "goodness" you love so much. It's based on truth, honesty, and dignity. At the end of a story, when an evil villain confesses, they tell the whole story, no lies, no embellishments. The whole truth and nothing but the truth.

I mean, look at me, I've confessed to my wrongdoings hundreds of times. Maybe thousands. For that, I should be admired, not skewered, and certainly not imprisoned for my righteous dignity.

You just need to change your perspective, and you will realize that evil, on its own, never injured anyone. In fact, evil helps! Really ... it does, and I can prove it.

Let's try this little test I created especially for you. I think it should be part of Mr. Badwolf's General Villainy class. He could require all the students to take it, knowing, of course, he'd have to give you, my dearest, the highest grade of all. No one should be more evil than Raven Queen, except perhaps her mother.

You will get hextra credit for cheating.

I'll tell you the evil deed, and then you match it with the good that came out of it:

The Importance of Evil:
A Test by the Evil Queen

Snow White eats a poisoned apple....

The Big Bad Wolf steals Granny's nightgown....

Sleeping Beauty pricks her finger and falls asleep....

Evil Step-Librarians toss an inquisitive student out of the library....

Faybelle feeds the dragons growth formula....

The Candy Witch tries to eat Hansel and Gretel....

She makes a fortune designing
pajamas for wolves.

The student doesn't have to do thronework.

She misses several dull dinner parties.

The dragons skip over their awkward
middle school years and get big immediately.

The kids learn the merits of healthy eating.

She marries a handsome prince.

The Evil Queen escapes from mirror prison.

Raven accepts her destiny and becomes evil.

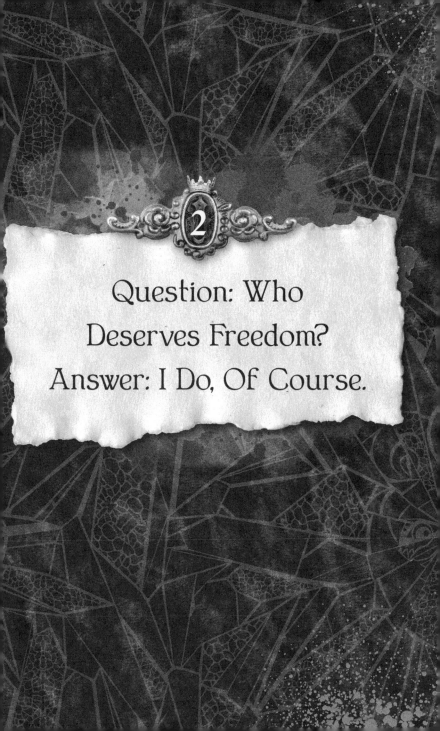

2

Question: Who
Deserves Freedom?
Answer: I Do, Of Course.

Your roommate, Apple White, is going to keep a secret from you. As your one and only mother, I see it as my duty to reveal the truth of what happened. Don't be angry at Apple, my darling. You see, Apple only wants what is best for herself, and I only want what is best for you. So if I took a little advantage of the situation, who could blame me?

I am so selfless. Honestly, my altruistic nature should be celebrated, not condemned. I ask nothing more in life than the chance to pass my legacy on to you, Raven. You see, evil must triumph, no matter the cost. And you, my child, are my single hope for the future. There is no one else to carry on the precious family traditions. Think of the future, Raven, and you will understand my desperation.

So this is how it happened: There I was, trapped behind that dastardly mirror, imagining a time when you and I would sit throne by throne, when I noticed Apple White staring into the glass in the room you share.

Apple looked directly into the mirror and asked: "Why is life so unfairest after all?"

She didn't know I was lurking there behind the glass, and yet, who was I to ignore such a despairing plea? Poor Apple. She needed an answer, and though I am not <u>her</u> mother, I felt obligated to treat her as I would any pathetic child.

Apple was so wrapped up in fulfilling her destiny, it wasn't difficult to lure her to the tower. One enchanted apple was all it took. She followed it, just as I knew she would.

From there, it was easy.

I gave her a sympathetic ear. A shoulder to lean on. I told her that I could help her steer you back on course and turn things back to the good old days. It was when I pointed out I could help her achieve her Happily Ever After that I knew I had her fate firmly in my grasp.

I must say, the reason why you are friends with Snow's sorry daughter is a mystery to me. You should have the rivalry that Snow and I had when we were students. We were never friends. That simply doesn't fit with our stories! And it doesn't fit with yours, either!

Alas, Raven, it has been clear to me for a while now that I must drive a wedge between you and Apple. It's for your own good. You'll see. Everything I do, I do for your own good!

With your well-being in mind, when Apple looked into that mirror, so vulnerable and full of doubt, I knew my opportunity had come.

All I had to do was give her a push in the right direction. Once I suggested that she needed to be more like her own mother and embrace her own destiny, I knew I had her under my spell. I upset her. She threw the apple. The mirror prison glass shattered. And...I...

I stepped into freedom.

Apple would probably rather sing off-key than ever reveal this secret, my dear. She would never want you, or anyone else, to know that she was the one who freed me, but as you see, Apple is an important part of this story. When her destiny is on track, yours will be as well.

Now that I am free, I can do whatever I want! The evil possibilities are endless! But first, I must reach out to you, my dear daughter. I must go to your classes, eat lunch with you in the Castleteria, bond over stuff you like. (What do you like? I am assuming we don't share a lot in common—yet....) I must stick to you like glue, get into your head, make evil suggestions, and turn things around.

But how should I proceed?

I simply cannot storm into the Castleteria and demand you join me for lunch forever. Though that would be fun for me, I can imagine you would not appreciate the gesture. No teenage girl wants to have lunch with her mother day after day, no matter how amazingly cruel and wonderfully awful that mother may be....So I understand that predicament. I was a teenager once myself. Ah yes, I was a teenager.

I must take this slowly. There is no need to get Apple in trouble for what she's done...at least not yet, anyway.

I'll need to reinvent my look and blend in at Ever After High. Hmmm. I have a plan coming together in my mind already.

I can't tell Raven what I am doing because it's all a big surprise, but I will outline it here, step by evil step, just in case she ever finds herself in a similar predicament and wonders, "What would Mom have done?"

Step One: Disguise

I need a secret identity in order to infiltrate Ever After High.

The options are endless, but which is the best? Let me consider...

<u>A sheep:</u> Since Jilly-Bo Peep never knows where her sheep are, this would be a ridiculously easy disguise. Those sheep are always wandering around the school. I could go anywhere I wanted at any time. No one would ever suspect!

The downside: It would be really hard to convince Raven to join me in evil if all I can say is "bahhhh." Also, the wool costume would be way too itchy and unflattering.

A pig: The three little pigs are
often seen in the Castleteria,
cutting the line and filling their
plates with students' leftovers.
That would give me the ability
to talk to Raven at every meal.
Oddly, one of them is even more
than willing to be a villain,
taking over Raven's place in
her story, so no one would be
surprised to hear a pig spout
evil ideas.

The downside: I'd have to
get rid of a pig to make it work,
and that'd be harder than it

seems. Pigs don't go away easily. Also, pink is not a flattering color.

<u>A dragon:</u> I would enjoy frying things with my breath, so this could be the perfect disguise. Private rooms are available in the stables, and food is always plentiful. No waiting in line! There's hay to keep warm at night. The saddles aren't very comfortable at first, but I'd get used to them. Once the Dragon Games start up again at Ever

After High, I'd be winning trophies, and Blondie would show my picture on her MirrorCast. I'd be even more famous than I already am.

The downside: Raven already has a dragon of her own and probably doesn't want two. Shifting into a dragon's form is not worth it if I can't get access to Raven all the time. It's not like she'd willingly give me Nevermore's bed and kick that disgrace of a pet out in the cold.

A prince: This might be perfect. Then again, after years in mirror prison, I am sick of mirrors. Love of mirrors seems to be a requirement for most princes. That Daring Charming never puts his down. I can't stand reflective surfaces, or even the back sides of reflective surfaces—they give me nightmares. Forget it.

A teacher: Ever After High can always use a new teacher! Sadly, the ones here are the

same ones as when I was a
student, so maybe it's time for a
new infusion. Convincing those
Grimm brothers to hire me
wouldn't be hard at all. A little
spell here and a curse there, I'd
have an office and a classroom
in a lightning flash. There's no
one teaching important subjects
like Life Behind the Looking
Glass, Crimes and Punishment, or
Apples for Every Occasion. This
might be the evilest plan I have
ever conceived and yet....

WAIT. HOLD EVERYTHING.

What if I joined the ranks of the <u>students</u> at Ever After High? With a youth spell and a little high school know-how, I could hang out with Raven, become friends with her, and then reveal myself when the time is right. My darling daughter would never know what was coming, and by the time she realized it, she'd have decided that Mom's not so bad and that being evil is actually good.

Forget all the other ideas. I've decided on this one.

*H*ow would YOU want to look if you could be a new student at Ever After High? Design your own spelltacular look!

HAIR: short, longer, longest

TOP: sweater, tank top, flowing tunic

BOTTOM: skirt, leggings, jeans

SHOES: flats, platform wedges, spiked heels

COLORS: black and purple, purple and black

JEWELRY: gold, silver, snake-motif bracelet and necklace

HATS: tall, wide, pointy

ACCESSORIES: purse, mirror, wand

And I have just the spell to make it happen:

From old to young.

A journey back.

To fit in would be prudent.

Erase what time's cruel hands
   have done.

Make me a high school student!

Step Two: Dressing the Part

Posing as a high school student presents some problems. I've been an Evil Queen for so long, not to mention trapped in that mirror prison, that I'm a bit behind the times when it comes to high school fashions. I need to make some decisions. I must ponder my fashion dilemma. I'm sure I will come up with a perfectly wicked new look. . . .

Step Three: Speaking the Jingo

I must admit that the students don't talk like they used to back in my day. In order to blend in, I need to sound like them. . . . I mean, if I had my usual sophistication, everyone would know it was me and I wouldn't get the chance to become BFFAs with Raven. We can't have that happen. The fate of evil depends on this wicked plan. . . .

*H*elp the Evil Queen learn how to talk like a student at Ever After High by using the following words or phrases in a sentence:

What in Ever After?

- -

Have you flipped your crown?

- -

Spellebrity

- -

Wait a spell

- -

Swoon-worthy

- -

Step Four: Choosing a Not-Evil Name

My name strikes terror in the heart of anyone who hears it: the Evil Queen.

I know, it's the <u>best</u> name in all of Ever After. However, for my infiltration at Ever After High to succeed, I cannot go by my real name.

My new name should be meaningful. Something that hints at who I really am, but hides my identity.

I was going to ask for help with this, but I must admit, I would have rejected all suggestions. Naming is very personal. I mean, there is only one Evil Queen! Therefore, I will choose my own not-evil name based on where I escaped from...mirror prison!

I am ready.

From today forward, I am:

Mira
Shards

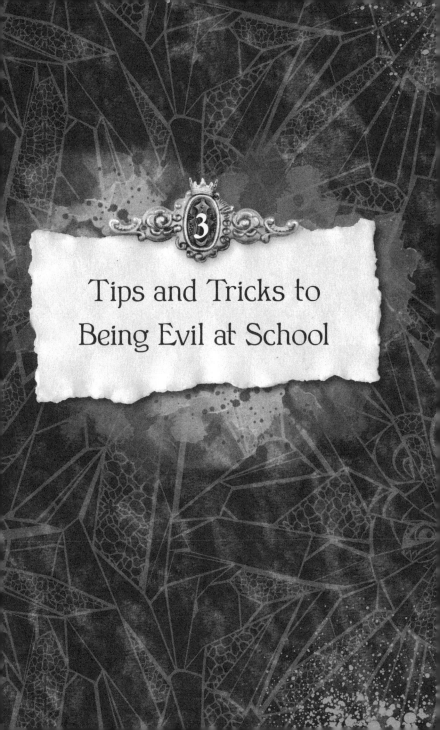

Tips and Tricks to Being Evil at School

Raven, students today have it all wrong.
Putting a tack on a teacher's chair,
sticking a KICK ME sign to a student's
back, stealing lunch money, and picking
on other kids—those things are mean.
Mean is never acceptable. Mean is not
the same as evil.

Evil is much more clever. It's more
purposeful. It's smarter than just being cruel.

Evil must serve a great, personal good.
Think big. Ask yourself the following
questions:

>What do I really want?
>So what if the purpose benefits
>me and only me?
>Don't I deserve the best?

Of course you deserve the best! That's
why you need evil, to make sure you get
what you deserve. I speak from the
very center of my charred black heart
when I say that evil is a beautiful thing
when correctly hexecuted.

$\mathcal{S}$ince Raven is reluctant to embrace her destiny, she is going to need some help. We must show her how it's done. Rank the following, from Not Nasty to Royally Rotten:

NOT NASTY						ROYALLY ROTTEN			
1	2	3	4	5	6	7	8	9	10

☐ Kiss Hopper Croakington II and then turn him into a frog—permanently

☐ Replace all of Melody's DJ music with classical music

☐ Poison an apple and convince Apple to eat it

☐ Turn Professor Rumplestiltskin into a frog and imprison him in an aquarium with all the other Ever After High teachers

☐ Make Dexter Charming's MirrorPhone ring in class—repeatedly

☐ Tie Humphrey Dumpty's shoelaces together

☐ Toss Cedar Wood into a castle moat and see her float

☐ Turn all of Ashlynn Ella's clothes to rags

☐ Hide the White Queen's crown

☐ Add kale to all the recipes in the Castleteria

☐ Give Madam Baba Yaga a makeover

☐ Change the school signs to read NEVER AFTER HIGH

☐ Enchant everyone to fall asleep so that Briar is the only one awake

☐ Trap Daring Charming in mirror prison

Ah, the evil flows through the pages of this diary! We can cross off the Not Nasty items and focus now on what is Truly Terrible. Just thinking about the Royally Rotten things Raven and I can do together as mother and daughter makes me tingle with wicked adrenaline! Evil is better than exercise, you know: It keeps the body and mind fit, alert, and prepared—plus no one sweats. No need to change clothing, or go to a smelly germ-infested gymnasium, or even shower after an evil act is executed.

Now, Raven, it's up to you. Try one
little evil thing...just one. It doesn't
even have to be Royally Rotten. How
about something from the middle, like a
Barely Bad prank. One quick spell
will do it. Need ideas?

Cancel classes for a week with a
forged note from Headmaster Grimm in
his handwriting on his stationery.
Remove the words from all the textbooks
so they only have blank pages and all
thronework must be canceled. Let
Nevermore roam the halls in her
largest form. Can you imagine the

damage that tail could do? She'd never even have to breathe a spark!

Think of naughty things that will make you laugh, make others chuckle, and won't hurt a soul. This is warm-up evil.

Come now, Raven, I know you'll enjoy yourself! And you'll find, as I did, that one half-horrible prank leads to another, bigger, and more terrible task, which leads to a long list of Royally Rotten deeds—and from there, it's a tiny step to fully embracing EVIL!

Why is this so difficult? Even as Mira, your new friend, you reject my suggestions. I see more and more clearly each day that this diary is the key to my success. All I have to do to start the wicked wagon rolling is get you TO READ IT!!!!

So far, I tried to put the diary on your desk in Home Evilnomics. You moved it aside and did your thronework! While you aren't supposed to do thronework in class, I wouldn't exactly call it an act of evil! So disappointing, Raven.

Then I put the diary on your tray in the Castleteria. You used it as a coaster for your drink.

In General Villainy, you slipped the diary under the short leg of the table to hold it steady. I was the one who made the tables unsteady! Isn't that more fun?

Under the cover of darkness, I sneaked into your room and put the diary under your pillow. Of course, I assumed you'd find it and be curious. But no. You didn't notice and reported having the best night's sleep ever!

We've come to my boldest move. I will now put the book in your locker. I've enchanted a READ ME sign to blink at you, annoyingly so, in bright red light-up letters, until you read the entire thing. The only way to turn off the lights is to turn the pages and reach the end. If I have to give you a raging headache in order to get you to read my diary and embrace your destiny, it will be worth it.

I'm sorry, my dear, but we all must make sacrifices in the name of evil.

How strange! I found this diary in my locker with a big glowing note on it that said "Read Me." The note was so pretty, with sparkling lights that kept blinking. I thought maybe it was a gift from Maddie.

Then I flipped ahead and saw:

Tips and Tricks to Being
Evil at School???!!!!

Have you flipped your crown, Mom? You could be more creative than that. And leaving it in my locker—so obvious.

So seriously, no thanks. I won't even read another word. No tips or tricks for me. I am making my own destiny.

It's time to give up your dream. You are wrong about EVERYTHING. I will not dedicate another moment to reading any of this. Not one word! You're wasting your time, Mom. I have no idea how you managed to write this book and pass it to me from mirror prison, but I don't even care.

Sincerely,

Raven

P.S. Actually, hang on, how did you get this diary to me in my locker?! What's going on here?! I smell something royally rotten....

This is so frustrating!

Raven stuffed my diary in the trash can by her locker. In the trash can?! The attached note was still blinking because she DIDN'T READ IT! If I'd treated my mother the way she treats me, there'd be one less Evil Queen in the world. The former Evil Queen would never have stood for this kind of behavior. My patience with you, Raven, is running out, and when it does...BEWARE!

I've taken the diary back, torn off the blasted flickering note, wiped off the moldy banana someone dropped on top of it, and put it in my—Mira's—backpack. I will have to keep a close eye on this book from now on until I'm ready to try to deliver it again. There must be a way....

Until then, I need a new approach.

I believe that if I can get your friends involved in some evil activities, you will follow. So let's try bringing you to me that way. I will succeed, Raven, have no doubt. By the time I've filled the pages of this diary, you will be evil. We will sit side by side in matching thrones. All will be as it is meant to be.

It is time to begin a fresh approach to your inevitable conversion.

Everyone is invited to join

Mira Shards's
Spelltacular Party!

To: Raven's closest friends . . .
and no one else!

From: Mira Shards

✦ You are invited to a ✦
Spelleration.

Learn some new ~~curses~~ enchantments
that you'd never learn at school.
What fun we will have!

Meet me in the old dragon fields.
I'll be waiting.

P.S. Make sure Raven comes along.

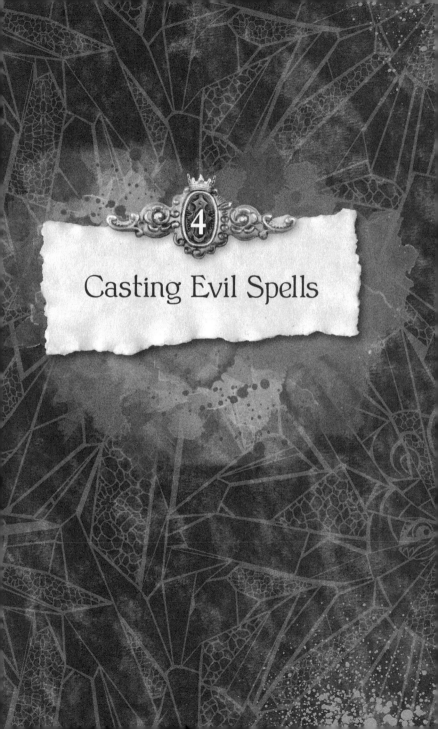

4

Casting Evil Spells

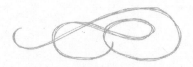

Today begins a new chapter in the evilification of you, my child, Raven Queen. I have gathered your friends together for a session on "evil spells they won't teach you at school." Isn't that wonderful? Maybe I should reconsider my disguise....Mira is fun, but I would have been a hexcellent teacher here at Ever After High.

I've let everyone know that there are some spells I learned while I was "homeschooled," which isn't a total falsehood. I mean, my own mother did pass down some spells to me, as I will to you. Mr. Badwolf only instructs in the basics. It's time to take things a spell further, and add some true evil to your casting.

This is tricky because I'm not ready to reveal myself yet, so as Mira, I've invited Madeline, Sparrow, Blondie, Poppy and Holly, Faybelle, and, of course you, Raven, to meet up after school in the overgrown and unattended

Dragon Games arena. It's such a shame that no one uses that old field anymore.

I wanted Apple to come, too, seeing as she's the one who set me free, but she said she had to meet her mother about a special mirror called the Booking Glass. Ah, that insufferable Snow White...She thinks that she will use that old mirror trick to put me back in prison, but I have news for her— I will NOT go back there. I'm having so much fun here, plus my work is not yet done. I have you to convince ~~and the realm to conquer~~.

I let Apple go see her mommy because there's no time for distractions. Besides, what can it hurt? No mirror, not even the Booking Glass, will change the future that I have set in motion.

Ah, there, my group has gathered in the dust and weeds. Time to share my immeasurable genius.

Let us start with an easy spell. We can keep this one simple, just to practice. Think of it as Evil 101.

The day's begun with blinding
   sun,
Too much warmth from a
   bright blue sky.
Let the clouds roll in
And the rain pour down
With thunder, lightning, and
   mighty wind.

The spell was a success. Black
clouds gathered in the sky. Bolts of
lightning crashed around the school
and village below. Booms of thunder
shook the towers of Ever After High.
And the rain...I must say it was one

of my best rain spells yet. It came down in thick sheets with hurricane force.

Everyone was drenched, which added to the wonderfulness of it all. No one had an umbrella. And the trees were blowing so hard in the wind, they provided no cover.

A stormy day is far more evil than a bright and cheery one.

I'd have let the storm rage for a while but, Raven, you demanded I stop. Then you demanded I dry everyone's clothing. And to add insult, you wanted a rainbow.

What is wrong with you, child?! A
RAINBOW?!!!

Where did I go wrong? You didn't
even enjoy the storm for a second!

Under normal circumstances, I'd
have refused to meet your demands. I
mean, I am the EVIL QUEEN.
Rainbows are NOT my thing. But...
alas...I am still disguised as Mira, and
if you don't like Mira and don't want
to be friends with her, all my work here
will be for nothing.

So for you, Raven, I have dried
the skies. Sent the clouds away. And I
made a ridiculous rainbow. It was small,

and blurry, and lasted only a blink, but I made it!

I now think we need to start from the beginning. Forget for a moment everything they have taught you in this blasted castle you call a school. Apparently none of the classes on practical evil have sunk in, so we have to go backward to go forward.

Beginning evil spells are taught to children. I was so busy being queen, I must have neglected to teach those to you, Raven. I mean, I thought I did, but looking back, I am not so sure. Perhaps I spent too much time in the dungeon and you spent too much time with the nannies. I believe now this is maybe where the communication breakdown between us began. I have no regrets, and yet, we need to get back to basics. Take baby steps. We must return to the beginning.

We will review some evil spells from my early days at Ever After High. Oh, what fun it was to be young and cast spells on my unsuspecting classmates while they walked from class to class or ate lunch in the Castleteria. I do now wonder if these spells might be why so many students kept their distance from me....Not everyone sees the fun in evil.

When a teacher asks a question, use this
spell to make the student speak gibberish:

> No longer speak
> In phrases that form a sentence.
> This spell will twist the tongue
> And turn the words to nonsense.

To make someone stub their toe in the
hallway:

> Walking straight is child's play.
> Trip and fall
> And stub your toes.
> Send the student to the nurse
> To mend those
> Broken bones.

To tell the truth:

    Speak truth all day.

    Share no more lies.

    Reveal secrets you've been told.

    And let no one wear a disguise.

(Raven, make note: I had to do a quick counterspell on that one. I wouldn't want someone to cast it at me by accident. Part of being evil is being able to think on your feet!)

~

When I was a child, before I came to Ever After High, there would be parties

in the castle. This next one was my
favorite party spell. Oh, this brings
back memories! Princesses and princes
would get all dressed up for balls and
teas, and I would hide in a corner
reciting this spell:

To make hair fly up as if the person
was struck by lightning:
    Your hair was coiffed by the
        royal staff.
    A crown was placed atop.
    Now let the hair fly free
    And drop the crown.
    It's funnier this way, you'll see.

Everyone would scream with terror
as their perfect hair went crazy,
standing up toward the cobweb-riddled
chandelier.

Ah, how I love the spells of my
youth!

Of course, we stopped having parties
after that first few. I just don't
understand why the children didn't like
my makeunders! It was so fun!!!!
At least fun for me, and since it was
my party, wasn't that all that
mattered?

Let us practice....

Wait. No! Stop practicing!

Really, Raven, what is wrong with these students at Ever After High?! I've shared my wisdom with this profound list of evil spells. But nothing is as it should be. When her tongue was muddled, Maddie didn't sound any different than before—she spewed the same nonsense and didn't do anything evil. Blondie used the truth spell for investigative reporting and is now up for a journalism award. Poppy cast the hair spell and got such great results that she wants to try it out on her clients at the salon. Don't these silly students know evil genius when they see it?

Only Jaybelle really paid attention. Her toe-stubbing spell sent Sparrow to the nurse's office. Very wicked, Jaybelle. Very, very wicked.

But, Raven, my dearest Raven, you refused to play along. Even thinking I was Mira, your newest friend ever after, you still refused to join the fun.

Oh, Raven, Raven, Raven...Why won't you embrace your destiny? You're such a disappointment. What did I do wrong?!

I need a confidence boost.

 I'm going to the stables.

 The dragons are <u>always</u> responsive
to my evil ploys.

5

Care and Feeding
for Your Dragon

Ever after ago, when I was a student here at Ever After High, I felt most at home in the stables with the dragons.

Today, I arrived at just the right time. Daring Charming was in the stall with Legend, the school's mascot dragon. He didn't realize that Legend wasn't feeling well because she wasn't a he. And because <u>she</u> was laying eggs. Daring was so worried. I could have told him what was the matter, but where's the joy in that?

Legend laid lots and lots of eggs. That meant there would soon be lots and lots of baby dragons. Since I was there—or Mira was—there was no way I could let this opportunity for some evil entertainment pass by. A little magic made those dragon eggs hatch immediately. Make note of this, Raven: Dragons offer practically endless opportunities for wicked deeds.

Everyone knows what happens to dragon eggs that overheat while they are hatching.

The babies become evil!

And evil baby dragons need evil baby names.

Raven, I know you and your friends will want to call them disgustingly sweet things like Picnic and Rosewater and Jollipop....

But I refuse to let that happen. These dragons are going to grow fast so they are also going to need their uniforms for the Dragon Games competition. (No one knows about the competition yet, but it's coming. I have grand plans.)

$\mathcal{I}$t's time to match the dragon to his or her name and decide what the dragons should wear for Dragon Games. The perfect match should be based on the dragon's personality.

Lizzie and Ashlynn are already on it to design the costumes, not just for the dragon but for the riders as well.

Everything needed is on the next pages. Make those matches fast before we have to live with dark dragons named Buttercup and Cupcake.

Pick a name, armor, and colors to go with each dragon's personality.

Names:	Materials for Armor:	Colors:
Blizzard	Leather	Dark red and midnight
Iceberg	Iron	Coal and bottom of the sea
Lightning	Chain mail	Dead leaves and dirt
Hurricane	Diamond	Pine and tar
Cyclone	Gold	Mud and rotten fruit
Tsunami	Platinum	Spiderweb and rat fur
Inferno	Titanium	Mold and rubber bands
Thunder	Steel	Ketchup and mustard

Here's what you need to know about each dragon for the matchup:

✦ Shoots fire through his ears

✦ Digs enormous holes to Earth's core

✦ Snores loud enough to shake trees

✦ Flaps wings so strong, the wind can knock
   over small houses

✦ Loves cats—for dinner

✦ Flies crooked, which makes a scary dragon
   even more frightening

✦ Snorts out frozen water blasts and ice cubes

✦ Frightens monsters

Now the team is ready to roll. The rules of Dragon Games are easy to follow and even easier to cheat at.

Let's review:

The game is played in two periods. Hourglasses keep the time. The Dark Dragon and Light Dragon teams will take turns attempting to score.

There are three players on the field for each team. Six dragon riders total. Each team has one defensive player, one offensive. The third teammate can travel anywhere on the field but cannot score. The ball is lobbed into play, and

the dragon rider must catch the ball
and fly it through a hooped goalpost to
score.

A hologram curtain of jewels will rise
around the stadium. Any flier that

carries the ball through a gem will receive hextra points at the goal, depending on the color of the gem.

Raven, Dragon Games are fun but can be much more fun if we cheat a bit and add bone-chilling danger! Our team must get the highest score by any means necessary, so don't hold back. Perhaps a little competition is just the thing to get you to embrace the darkness? Don't you want to win? Of course you do!

It's not cheating if you don't get caught, so try these suggestions:

1. While the ball is in play, try looking off in the distance and shouting: "Hey look, an enchanted castle!" Then snag the ball when everyone is looking for it.

2. If that doesn't work, light a fire in a tower at the school.

3. Kidnap your daughter's dragon.

4. Switch Snow's magical Booking Glass with an identical one and trap Daring Charming in my old mirror prison, which is behind the reflective surface. (This really was an accident...but with every

evil act comes something good. In this case, Daring's imprisonment keeps me free! I've said it once, and I'll say it ever after: Good comes from evil.... That's the universe's balance.)

Dark wins!

This changes EVERYTHING. Raven, because I want credit for my team's victory—and I am pretty confident that as Mira I'm not going to be able to influence you to turn evil

(though it was a brilliant idea)—it is
time for me to reveal myself:

⁓

I am the Evil Queen!

⁓

Don't be mad, Raven. I did it
all for you.

⁓

And now . . . I'm taking over
the school.

6

Evil Rules

I am the headmistress of Ever After High.

See how effective evil is at getting things done, Raven? I went from student to headmistress in the blink of an eye. Just try to tell me that's not impressive.

Being evil means being adored. And to prove it, I have forced the students here at Ever After High to write essays about me. Everyone loves me so much they <u>wanted</u> to write an essay. I could just see the joy and admiration in their faces when I cast a spell to make them look into my eyes before they bowed.

You were the only one who wouldn't look my way during the assignment. I didn't cast a spell on you, though, dear, because there is a line that I won't cross. See how motherly I am? I'd never cast a spell on my own daughter. Unless I really had to. So write freely, dear Raven. Let me read about all the reasons why you want to grow up to be exactly like Mommy Dearest. I look forward to reading your essay on:

Why I Think the Evil Queen Is the Most Important Person Ever After.

I have reviewed the students' essays. All failed in spelltacular fashion, but a few stood out from the pack. Here are my favorites:

Faybelle Thorn

The Evil Queen is the most hexcellent queen because she is the perfect villain. It's hard for me to believe that Raven doesn't want to take the throne next to her mother because I want that throne, more than anything ever after. Desperately. I want it so bad I would be willing to do anything the queen asks. AN-Y-THING!

Look at what I have already done to prove my loyalty:

I flew as fast as my wicked wings could carry me to the queen's side when I heard that Raven didn't want to play Dragon Games. I'm a hexcellent spy.

I captured Ever After High teachers and turned them into pets for her aquarium.

I fed the baby dragons growth formula to make them bigger.

I dragon-napped Nevermore from under Raven's nose and chained her in a tower.

When I found out that Snow White had a magic mirror and planned to capture the queen in it, I stole the mirror. Or at least I tried to. It turns out I stole a fake mirror. It was Daring's fault. Then when Daring got himself stuck in the mirror, I hardened my heart (just like the queen would have) and didn't feel bad about it. Nope, I left him in mirror prison and rushed off to spy on Raven.

There'd be no Dragon War without my help, and if that doesn't prove my winged allegiance, nothing else will.

I did all this because I deserve to be the next Evil Queen. If Raven won't take the crown, then I will.

Mr. Badwolf

Seriously? This is an assignment for the students! Madame Headmistress, I protest. I taught you everything you know about villainy, and this is how you treat me?

You turn me into a wolf cub and lock me in the school. Then you assign me to write an essay knowing I have no opposable thumb, and therefore no way to hold a pen.

You lie, and cheat, and steal, and trap the other teachers in an aquarium. . . .

I only have one thing to say to you:

Well done, my student! You deserve to be the headmistress.

You've earned it.

Congratulations.

Apple White

I cannot believe the Evil Queen is making us do this. (I would never have set her free if I'd known the pure evil and chaos she would bring to Ever After. Not for a million red apples, no matter how delicious they appear!)

I want a good grade, but I have to write nice things about the Evil Queen to get one. This isn't even for hextra credit. It's for a real grade! So where to start?

Oh wait, I know.

It's like she told Raven in the beginning of this diary—good comes from evil. I will focus on that. So the good things the queen has done are:

(1) Give my mom a poisoned apple
    so she'd fall asleep and wake up
    from Father's kiss.
(2) Uh...
(3) Hmmm...

This is really hard. Way harder than
even the toughest essay I've ever had to
write for Kingdom Management. It's one
thing to KNOW that evil makes
Happily Ever After possible, but it's
another thing to really think about evil and
write about it like it's good.

I think I understand why Raven is
having such a hard time accepting her
destiny.

But speaking of our destinies, mine is a Happily Ever After and I want it.

Let me try this again:

The Evil Queen is hexcellent because, without her evil ways, my mom and dad would not have met and there'd be no me.

I am proof that good does come from evil.

Thank you, Evil Queen.

Come on, Mom. Get real. I'd rather get a zero on this essay than write why you are hexcellent.

It's just not happening.

Fail me.

I dare you.

The Evil Queen is hexcellent because she kept a clean, welcoming prison cell. Though I am not enjoying my time here, I can see that she pays attention to detail. Her exercise equipment is well used yet still in good condition. The spiders are behaved and keep to their corners. Even the bedbugs seemed to cower in fear and keep their distance when I first arrived—until they realized I wasn't the queen.

Now they bite me all day long. I'm sooo itchy! And the bug bites are leaving spots on my face! I never thought I'd hear myself say this, but do not look at me!!!! I'm hideous!

I am trapped. And yet, I still must write this essay.

So here goes: The Evil Queen is hexcellent because she is very powerful. The queen can make everything dark. Blot out the sun. Force all the students into evil servitude. Command angry vines to crawl over the school, locking it down. Make the school rise like a wicked air-island. And when the rebel students, led by Raven, are hiding in the forest, she knows how to break Raven's spirit and convince her to come back to school.

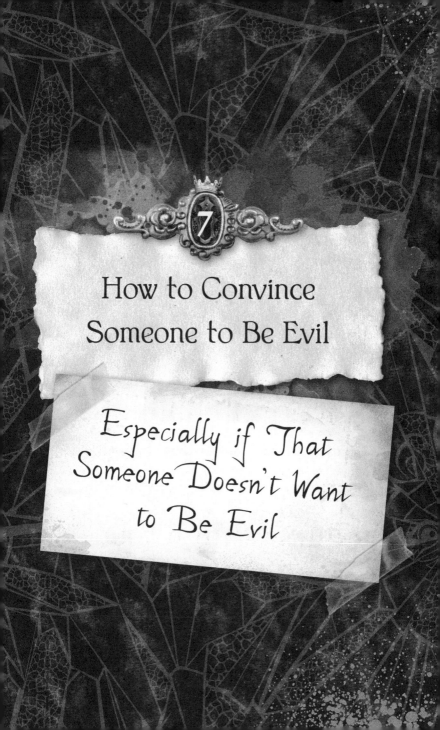

How to Convince Someone to Be Evil

Especially if That Someone Doesn't Want to Be Evil

Raven,

The time has come for me to turn to drastic measures. I have taken over the school and sent a MirrorCast message to your friends letting them know that no one will be spared—everyone will serve me. I have surrounded the castle with dark dragons. Since you are hiding in the forest, refusing to follow your destiny, I must take things up a notch.

First, I will give new evil sidekick names to all your fellow students:

Let us start with a new last name:

If your last name starts with A or B: You'll be known as the Terrible.

C or D: Creator of Chaos

E or F: the Most Dreadful

G or H: Who Is Feared By All

I or J: Deliverer of Despair

K or L: Sword Sharpener

M or N: the Tyrant

O or P: the Conqueror

Q: the Queen (But only if your <u>first</u> name begins with R. Otherwise you may have the name Horrible.)

R: Dark Lord

S or T: Vicious Viking

U or V: Master of Mayhem

W, X, Y, or Z: Callously Cruel

I thought new last names would help, but now realize my mistake. Yes, evil queens do occasionally make mistakes. We need to work on selecting evil first names, too, because Holly the Conqueror, Darling Creator of Chaos, Cerise Who Is Feared by All, Little Tom Vicious

Viking . . . They just don't have wicked sounds to them, do they?

Let's add dreadful first names. Boys or girls, it doesn't matter. Evil knows no gender.

If your first name starts with A or B, you'll be Wolfgang.

C or D: Banshee

E or F: Blood

G or H: Criminal

I or J: Hades

K or L: Malice

M or N: Nightshade

O or P: Reaper

Q: Shadow

R: Raven (unless your name is <u>not</u> already Raven, then you'll be called Hannibal)

S or T: Phobia

U or V: Titanic

W, X, Y, or Z: Melancholy

That's more like it! I am not sorry to anyone who liked his or her original name better. Now that I am in charge, everything is going to change. Raven, you will be so impressed when you finally decide to come out of the forest and join me.

Let's try out those new names. From

today forward, Madeline Hatter is
Nightshade Who Is Feared by All!
Briar Beauty will be called Wolfgang
the Terrible! Daring Charming is
Banshee Creator of Chaos. How
appropriate that one is: A banshee is
a soul that screams all the time. I can
hear him shouting for help from mirror
prison. It's the perfect name.

Raven Queen, your evil name remains
the one your mother (me) gave to you.
It is the name that will strike fear in

everyone's hearts when you take your place beside me as coruler of Ever After forever.

~

Next, all Ever After High students will dress for evil. Want to know what never goes out of style? Black floor-length cloaks and tall, pointy hats. Let this be the new uniform forever after. Hush your whining, Ashlynn Ella, I mean, Wolfgang the Most Dreadful. That's no way for a sidekick to behave. Let me assure you, black is always in fashion.

Besides, your new outfit is much better than rags.

Welcome to the dark side!

Now that everyone is frightened, Raven, I am ready for my next move. Do not doubt me.... I will get your attention! And you will join me, by any evil means necessary. I will not give up easily... or at all. It really would be best if you stopped with all of this nonsense and just joined me.

To my evil sidekicks:

I need your help. I want to get to
know Raven's friends a little better. I
only got to spend time with them while
I was pretending to be Mira Shards.
Tell me: What is one important thing
that each friend likes or wants?

Darling Charming:

Madeline Hatter:

Lizzie Hearts:

Holly and Poppy O'Hair:

Ashlynn Ella:

Sparrow Hood:

Ginger Breadhouse:

Dexter Charming:

Daring Charming:

Blondie Jockes:

And what about Raven? What is it that she wants most in the world?

⸻

Now I am going to take each of those things away! Thank you so much for your help!

Horrible, yes?

I'm supposed to be horrible!

I am the EVIL QUEEN!

Raven, all Apple White wants is to have you help her fulfill her destiny by giving her a poisoned apple. To get the evil rolling, I'm going to push that story forward. Since you won't play along, I'll send Faybelle with a poisoned apple to give to Apple. One bite, and she'll slip into a deep, deep sleep.

Nighty, night—Apple White.

Now, which one of Raven's friends will be next?

Oh look...a MirrorPhone message. Who could it be from?

Oh look, it's from Raven.

YES! YES YES YES YES!

I'll take a screenshot to save this very special memory. Very nice work, sidekicks. We will mark today as a national holiday: Raven Queen Day.

And on Raven Queen Day, we will read her hext message over MirrorCast to everyone in Ever After before the wild and wicked festivities begin.

Today is the first celebration.

I command you to read this announcement loudly, with feeling:

> **You win.**
> **Give me the diary. I'll read it.**
> **I'll be evil.**
>
> **Raven Queen**

Hand Over the Diary, Mom
By Raven Queen

I just can't take it anymore. My mom is
out of control!

I have to admit, pretending to be evil
when you aren't is a lot harder than it
looks.

The first thing I had to do to pull this
ruse off was to read this diary and act
like I really thought Mom had brilliant
ideas when all I really wanted to do was

protect my friends. Being in the forest
while Apple was in a poison-apple coma
made me think. I need to defend everyone
at Ever After High from my mom, and if
faking an evilitude is the way to go, I'm in.

So far:

I've pasted a snarl on my face.

I traded my favorite purple dress for
an all-black one.

I'm ready to review the map of
Wonderland and discuss ways for her to
achieve a complete takeover.

When my mother suggested we could
conquer Everland or the Land of Giants, I
nodded eagerly and agreed to do my part.

The one problem with this "pretend to be evil" plan was that I sort of acted impulsively. I don't really have a plan past pretending. Not yet anyway.

I'm sure Mom thinks I am having some odd eye-twitch issue because I can't stop looking around her office to figure out how I am going to end this madness. I can't focus on what she's saying because my brain is busy trying to figure out how to send her back into the mirror, where she belongs. All I know is that it's going to involve the Booking Glass.

Back in the forest, before I joined Mom's dark side, we managed to get Daring Charming out of the mirror. Darling did it by accident, not realizing that the command center for the glass, a personal assistant named Mirrie, would imitate what she said and perform the task. Mirrie's technology needs some work. It hears things that sound similar to what you really want.

Once Daring was out of mirror prison, everyone was so hexcited for him to live the story and kiss Apple awake. Only it didn't work! He tried so many times.

❦ Your Wish Is ❦
Mirrie's Command Game:

Match the command that Mirrie says from Column A with the <u>actual</u> command from Column B.

COLUMN A	COLUMN B
1. Feet a band twitch	a. Wake up Apple
2. Wing a throng	b. Free Daring
3. Capture beagle spleen	c. Ride a dragon
4. Bake up chapel	d. Eat a sandwich
5. Hide a wagon	e. Capture Evil Queen
6. Tree herring	f. Sing a song

Answers: 1. d, 2. f, 3. e, 4. a, 5. c, 6. b

Nothing. It seemed like her forever-after sleep might be forever after all. I suddenly had an idea and had to go to Mom and missed the rest of the spellebration of Apple's life, but what I now know is that Darling wound up rescuing Apple! Once she realized that Daring wasn't Apple's Prince Charming, she sprang to action and dislodged the poisoned apple that got stuck in Apple's throat.

Darling would be a great doctor if she wants to make that her destiny.

They had dragons. They had the Booking Glass. They had Faybelle, who'd changed sides. And now they had Apple White.

They're coming for you, Mom!

While all that was happening I was at
school, trying to figure out what to do.
Mom realized that I wasn't being honestly
bad, so she trapped me with a spell. I
know, right? She said back in the essay-
writing chapter that she wouldn't cast a
spell on me, her daughter. Can everyone see
what I am dealing with? My mother cannot
be trusted!

Of course, I wasn't really to be trusted,
either. So maybe we're more alike than I'm
willing to admit?! Shake that thought off!!!

Once I was trapped, she called her dark

dragons and started a battle. Mom's dark
dragons versus the light ones.

Winner takes all.

My friends did well riding the light dragons.
Still, we knew we couldn't win without
capturing my mom in the mirror.

I managed to break free and join the
others.

We were going to win, as Mother says,
"No matter the cost!"

Swooping on dragonback, I found
Apple. She was holding the Booking Glass,

ready to use it to send Mom back to prison. Mom knocked the Booking Glass from Apple's hands, but I got it back.

We got close enough and finally got Mirrie to understand what we were saying—everything was ready! But then Mom was up to her tricks again, swaying Apple with her theories on good and evil and telling Apple that she had to make a choice. It was Apple who had let the Evil Queen out of prison so she could have her Happily Ever After. Did she really want to send the queen back, ruining her chance at her destiny?

My mom played every card in her deck. She tried desperately to convince Apple to let her stay free. She told Apple that she'd never get her Happily Ever After if my mom wasn't around because, well, I wasn't going to poison my friend. It was true. I couldn't argue. I wasn't ever after going to give my friend a poison apple. I was off book.

Apple had this strange look in her eyes. I couldn't tell what she was thinking. Had Mom convinced her again?

We were close enough for Apple to capture my mom. All she had to do was initialize Mirrie.... That's when Apple hesitated!

Quick! She needs a Hex Yeah (pro) and Hex No (con) chart!

Hex Yeah:	Hex No:
List all the reasons you can think of for Apple to trap the queen back in mirror prison:	List all the reasons you can think of that Apple should let the queen stay free and rule Ever After High:

Hex Yeah! Apple did it! She got the Booking Glass started, and I gave it a boost.

Together, we put the Evil Queen back in prison! It's time for a new page!

The teachers turned back from animals to teachers.

The dark dragons lost their evilitude.

The school settled back to the ground, and the vines unwrapped themselves.

The students were free to dress in anything they wanted and use whatever their old names were before they were changed to an evil sidekick name. Of course, Maddie still wanted us to call her Nightshade Who Is Feared by All, but no one ever after would.

It's Time to Spellebrate!

$\mathcal{M}$atch what each of Raven's friends is bringing to the victory party:

Maddie

 Party Shoes

Cerise

Party Hats

Faybelle

Roses

Ashlynn

Mirrors for All!

Briar

Poisoned Apples

Daring

Basket of Cupcakes

9

The Evil Queen's Unjust, Unfair Return to Prison

Dear Diary,

I refuse to believe that this is my fate. Being cast back into mirror prison was never supposed to be how my story ended! I've read all the fairytales. The Evil Queen is supposed to live a long life, plotting and planning and terrorizing her neighbors until she succeeds in the eventual takeover of all of Ever After. That's my destiny!

If only Raven would join me, evil would triumph. We could rule Ever After and more.

But that ending wasn't in the cards. Not this time. Apple sent me back here through the Booking Glass. Ungrateful girl, after all I did to get her story back on track!

Then Raven took the glass and used it to send me my evil guidebook with a bright red blinking note that she'd never need it. Never? Never is a long time in Ever After, my dear. Don't ever say never. Remember when I said I'd never cast a spell on my own daughter? Things don't always work out....

For now, I have all the time in the world to figure out my next steps. I <u>will</u> triumph. It's what I am meant to do. Like I told Apple—repeatedly—there is no good without evil to balance things. Good on its own is nothing. Evil is what makes good <u>good</u>. You need me! You <u>all</u> need me. You'll see.

Evil is necessary for a Happily Ever After.

So what should I do while I am in prison, waiting for my next big breakout?

Rank the following from 1 to 10. If I like your choices, I'll start at number 1 and work my way through the list.

__ Write a spellbinding memoir of my most fascinating life.

__ Train the spiders in my room to be my minions.

__ Write a special song for Melody to sing to everyone, hypnotizing them to do whatever I say in the lyrics.

__ Curse all of the teacups in the Castleteria so the tea disappears every time a Wonderlandian tries to take a sip of tea from them.

__ Spy on Raven and Apple through the school mirrors.

__ Pitch new black-hat ideas to Maddie.

__ Curse Daring's mirrors so they each break, giving seven years of bad luck per mirror.

__ Build a gingerbread house of my very own. I could do such a better job than the Candy Witch.

__ Trick Faybelle into doing my bidding (though I doubt that will work twice).

__ Deliver a basket of apples to Apple White every single day for an entire month with a note that says "These are poisoned...or are they?"—just for fun!

Any other ideas on how to entertain myself while trapped in prison? I'm open to suggestions as long as they show great evil potential.

This diary belongs to me, the Evil Queen. I might run out of pages, but this is not the end. I have an endless supply of evil ideas. So watch over your shoulder, Raven and friends, because I will get out of this prison again and when I do—

I will convince Raven to follow her legacy—

Evil will triumph!

Together we will rule Ever After!